"Huh?" Cyclops stood there stunned, uncomprehending. He had thought they would be overjoyed to be rescued, happy that he had come back for them. He certainly hadn't expected this!

"You fool!" Angel shouted. "Don't you understand? *It* wanted you to come back—and bring others with you! It was all a trap—and now it's too late!"

Cyclops stared around him at the ruins of the collapsed building. Even as he watched, the earth seemed to slowly swallow the remaining rubble. And now, the horrifying truth was beginning to dawn upon him. Now, when it was indeed, as Angel had said, too late...

X-MEN

Second Genesis

adapted by Paul Mantell and Avery Hart

cover illustration by Dana and Del Thompson

text illustrations by Aristides Ruiz

adapted from a comic by Len Wein

Bullseye Books

Random House ⌂ New York

X-MEN

Second Genesis

Prologue

Outside the isolated estate, the rain came down in torrents. Bolts of lightning crackled, illuminating the towers of the old mansion hidden in the wooded hills of Westchester County, New York. Thunder rumbled ominously across the sky, as if the heavens themselves were aware of the danger.

Deep within the recesses of the cavernous building, in a room with no windows, a place so hidden that no sound of the tempest could be heard, sat a man in a wheelchair. No, not just a man—a mutant! His brilliant mind harbored telepathic powers unmatched any-where on the face of the earth.

He was bald, with intense ice-blue eyes that bespoke a world of trouble. He sat alone, star-ing at the amazing computer he had created. Cerebro, as he called it, could detect mutant activity anywhere on earth, and even beyond, for that matter.

A series of beeps and clicks signaled that Cerebro was making its calculations. The man came to attention, grabbing the readout as fast as the machine could spit it out.

"Ah, yes...excellent," the man said, nod-ding slowly. He swung his wheelchair around, only to find that he was no longer alone.

"I didn't hear you come in," he said to the red-visored figure who now stood solemnly before him.

"Your mind must have been on other things," the visored figure suggested.

"Yes, that's true," the bald man said, nod-ding. He looked down at the readout in his strong hands. It showed a map of the world, with seven pinpoints highlighted. Seven points of incredible power. Seven mutants...

"I must go now," he said, folding the read-out and putting it safely in his pocket. "Get the Blackbird fueled and ready. I *must* find them—at once. The danger is great—and there's not a moment to lose!"

CHAPTER ONE

THE MISSION

Winzeldorf, Germany, a tiny village nestled deep in the Bavarian Alps, had changed very little over the centuries. Life there was gentle and peaceful, with little to disturb the tranquil pace.

Little, that is, until now. For on this night, under the light of the full moon, came a mob armed with torches, townspeople who before had never even thought of violence. But tonight, they had murder on their minds.

"This way, *Herren!* The monster went this way!" shouted the man who led the mob. The angry crowd followed him down the narrow lanes of the village, chasing the beast that walked on two legs.

Kurt Wagner ran ahead of them, keeping to the shadows whenever possible. Monster, was it? he thought, stung by the word. He had been different since the day he was born, but that didn't make him a monster, did it? He had tried to live with the townspeople in peace, to show them that he meant no harm. But their narrow minds could not make room for the likes of him. Not ever. And now they meant to get rid of him once and for all.

With his blue fur, yellow eyes, three fingers on each hand, birdlike three-toed feet, and long tail that came to a sharp point at the end, Kurt Wagner knew he could never be like the others.

Perhaps things would have been simpler—and safer—if he'd stayed with *der Jahrmarkt*. But the life of a carnival freak was not for him.

What fools, he thought bitterly, looking back at the mob chasing close behind him. It was *they* who were the monsters, with their mindless prejudices, their unreasoned fears.

"Let them come if they must—let them try

to kill me," he said aloud, coming up against a stone wall that marked the end of the street. The *dead* end.

He was trapped, and he knew it. "At least if I die, it will be with courage!" he promised himself.

Turning his back to the mob, he sprung into an astonishing leap, which took him high enough to grab onto the roof of the nearest house. With a grunt, he pulled himself up, and stood looking down at the mob.

"We've got him now!" came an exultant voice from below him. "Come down, monster! Come down or we'll burn you down!"

Kurt Wagner opened his mouth to speak, but the hideous howls that issued from deep within him made it clear to one and all that whatever he was, he was not human.

"Go away, you fools!" he cried out. "I have done nothing wrong! Nothing that would hurt any of you!"

The only answer he received for his pleading was a dozen torches hurled his way. The thatched roof around him burst into flame.

Startled, Kurt looked at the nearby rooftops. In seconds, they too would be ablaze. He stared down at the mob below, his anger almost transformed to pity.

These people were insane—utterly insane, he realized. They were so filled with hatred and fear that they would risk destroying their entire village just to make certain that they destroyed him!

And for what reason? He had come among them to learn, yet all he had learned were the ways of blind, unreasoning violence. Well, if that was all that those who dwelt in the "normal" world had to teach him, he would show them now that he had learned his lessons well.

With another astonishing leap, Kurt Wagner swooped down on his attackers, smashing into their midst, his fists and feet flying. Howling wildly, he plunged through the thick of the mob, laying low one attacker after another, until the sheer weight of the mob's numbers carried him down.

"We have him! We have him!" shouted the crazed villagers. "Quick! Bring the stake! Now, monster, we will be rid of you. Now we will—"

"STOP!" Remarkably, at the sound of the command, the villagers froze in their tracks—literally. Not one of them moved a muscle!

But where had the commanding voice come from? Kurt Wagner looked around and saw a bald man in a wheelchair staring down at him, a worldly-wise smile on his face.

"What—how—what happened to them?" Kurt stammered, uncomprehending.

"I happened to them," the stranger answered. "My name is Charles Xavier. I heard you tell yourself you'd come here to learn. Well, my friend, I am a teacher. I run a school for gifted youngsters such as you—a school for mutants!"

"Mutant?" Kurt repeated slowly. "Yes...I have heard the word."

"*You* are a mutant, Kurt, and I can help you find your true potential. I offer you refuge...and purpose." The man was smiling compassionately at Kurt, staring into his very soul.

"Are you saying you can help me to be normal?" Kurt asked, his feelings a blur.

"Normal?" the professor repeated as he looked around at the frozen mob. "After what happened here tonight," he said, "do you think you truly want to be normal?"

"Perhaps not," Kurt answered. "I want only to be a whole Kurt Wagner. If you can help me be that, teacher...I will gladly follow you anywhere."

In Quebec, Canada, lay a secluded military installation. Few people knew of its existence—fewer still knew of its true purpose. The base was the home of a special government agency and its very special agent—the agent code-named Weapon X, but better known to his colleagues as Wolverine.

General Bradford's aide now walked up to the agent, careful to avoid his well-known temper, and even more careful to avoid the potentially dangerous consequences of that temper...

"Excuse me, sir," the aide said. "They're waiting for you in the conference room."

"Let them wait," growled Weapon X, his

eyes glowing white beneath his black and yellow mask. "It's good for the soul," he added, breaking into a crooked grin. Brushing past the terrified aide, Wolverine strode toward his destination.

"All right, gents," he announced as he entered the conference room. "I'm here. Now, who's this bigwig you want me to meet?"

"I am the bigwig, Wolverine," said a bald man in a wheelchair, a man who looked at Wolverine with eyes that burned right through him. "Professor Charles Xavier, at your service."

Wolverine looked the man up and down. "Am I supposed to be impressed?" he asked with his usual bravado.

But before the man in the wheelchair could answer, General Bradford broke in. "Apparently," he said, "the top brass is impressed, Wolverine. All I know is that the professor is here to make you some sort of an offer."

"An offer, eh?" Wolverine repeated, intrigued. "Okay, prof—you've piqued my curiosity. What's the deal?"

"I'll come straight to the point," said the

professor, his tone and gaze serious, even grave. "I know of you, and of your powers. You, my friend, are a mutant—and I have need of mutants. Desperate need."

"But what about my position here...?" Wolverine asked, confused.

"I'm offering you a chance to become a free agent," the professor replied at once. "A chance to learn how to put your powers to their greatest use!"

Wolverine's mouth curled into a smile. The professor, knowingly or not, had spoken directly to his deepest wish. "A chance to get out from under the red tape and rigmarole, eh?" he asked. "All right, professor...you've found your man!"

"What?" General Bradford sputtered, taking a step forward toward the two of them. "Not so fast, fella! The government has invested a great deal of time and money turning you into what you are now! You try walking out on us, and I'll have you locked up!"

Wolverine's smile vanished and he strode slowly toward the general, backing him right up against the wall.

"Sorry," he said, slowly, menacingly. "It seems you didn't get my meaning, friend. This is still a free country, isn't it?" And with that, he raised his hand and a razor-sharp adamantium claw emerged from his glove. It shined harshly in the light.

"So I'm resigning my commission," Wolverine growled, lifting his gleaming claw high in the air. "Effective immediately!"

With a lightning-fast stroke, he brought his hand down, the claw slicing neatly through the general's tie and cutting it in two.

Now Wolverine brought the claw up against the general's chin, backing him up even closer

against the wall, and added, "Do you have any further objections?"

"I think not," the general said, his eyes cast downward at the glinting weapon.

Turning, Wolverine grabbed the handles of the professor's wheelchair and guided him out of the room. Once through the door, he turned to face the general again, flashing him a broad smile and giving a little wave.

"Believe me, mister," said Bradford, frowning as he fingered the remaining half of his tie, "you haven't heard the last of this."

Wolverine laughed out loud. "Any time you want me," he said, "you know where to come looking! Come on, Professor—let's go. Nobody stops Wolverine once he's made up his mind to do something. *Nobody*."

And with that, Weapon X and Professor X departed together.

Things were going well so far, the professor reflected, as he and Wolverine boarded the special stratojet called the Blackbird that had brought him here to Canada. But there was still much traveling to be done. And his new team of mutants could not afford to lose even one of its seven prospective members. Not yet, before their mission had even begun…

Nashville's Grand Ole Opry was packed that evening, as usual, but that didn't matter to Professor Charles Xavier. He wasn't there to hear the country music bands that were playing that night. He was there to see someone in the audience—someone he knew quite well.

"Banshee!" he whispered, seeing the handsome blond man—or rather, mutant—sitting in the aisle seat ahead of him.

"Begorra!" the man said under his breath at the sight of his old mentor. His Irish brogue trilled off his tongue, reminding the professor of better days. "'Tis Professor X himself now!"

"Shhhh!"

The annoyed looks of the other spectators told the professor they were holding their conference in the wrong place. "Banshee, I must talk with you," he said, letting his Irish friend know by his tone that the matter was urgent.

Nodding, Banshee rose and guided the professor out of the hall, down the street to his shabby living quarters. He could not afford many luxuries these days.

Once the door was safely closed behind them, the professor quickly explained the nature and purpose of his visit.

"So that's the story, is it?" asked Banshee when Professor Xavier had finished his tale. "Then sure an' I'll help ye, Professor. 'Twill be nice to tread the straight an' narrow."

"Thank you, Banshee," Professor X said, allowing himself a small smile of relief. "I knew I could count on you. Meet me at Headquarters. I'll be there as soon as I round up the others. Oh, and one more thing..."

"Yes, Professor?" the blond mutant asked, his Irish eyes twinkling.

"Wish me luck, Banshee. I'll need it."

CHAPTER TWO

TO THE ENDS OF THE EARTH

On a hot and still afternoon, the tribespeople mounted the hundreds of stone steps that led to the altar at the top of the mountain. Each bore a gift in his hands—gifts for the goddess, Ororo, in hopes that she would bring them the rain that was so sorely needed.

Here in Kenya, East Africa, it had not rained for many months, and the crops were withering in the fields. Only Ororo could save the tribe from famine.

The elders of the tribe reached the great

stone portal of the goddess, their voices raised in praise and song—and prayerful supplication. "Ororo, great goddess of the storm," they cried, "come unto us and ease our burden!"

And with a hollow peal of thunder and the moan of lonely winds, the storm goddess appeared! Her white hair flowed down over her shoulders and covered her brown body. Arcs of lightning-like electrical current surrounded her as she stood facing them, her crystal-blue eyes searching theirs, reading their thoughts.

"I am here, my children," she announced. "What do you wish of me?"

"There is drought upon the land, blessed one," said the chief. "Our crops wither, our grasses parch. Ten goats and chickens shall we slay in your honor—if you will only bring us rain!"

The goddess's eyes, older than time, sparkled as she answered. "Save your beasts, my children. You need them more than I. All you need to do, you have done. Go home to your families, and give thanks. Tell the children I will do as you have asked."

Her liquid eyes grew dark then, and the sky grew dark as well. Once more, the howling winds came up and swept the storm goddess away. She soared aloft like an ebony bird, lightning lancing from her fingertips, the glow of life shining full upon her face.

She was happy here—truly happy only here, among nature's elements. The raging sky wept, touched by the electric charge of that great happiness. And the rains came...

When the storm goddess returned to earth at last, her joy was shared by all. The tribespeople burst into grateful song and began to dance, their bodies glistening with the long-hoped-for rain that beat down upon them. The goddess stood back, her arms folded across her chest, pleased that her people were happy.

"A most impressive display, Ororo...truly beautiful."

Ororo turned, startled at the voice, which spoke to her in English, the language of her early childhood. A language she had not heard in many years...

The memories came flooding back—memo-

ries of her parents. Her father, the American photojournalist; her mother, the Kenyan princess. Ororo had been born in Harlem, in New York City, but when she was a baby her parents had taken her to Egypt, where her father had been posted to cover the fighting near the Suez canal.

There, Ororo's parents had been killed and Ororo herself had nearly perished when a fighter plane crashed, instantly reducing their apartment building to a pile of rubble.

The orphaned girl had been taken in by a gang of thieves, and within a year she had become the most accomplished child beggar-thief in Cairo. But something, some inner voice, kept calling her southward, toward the land of her ancestors.

Finally, she could resist no longer. For more than a year she walked, until she came to the land she knew instinctively was her own. There, she had grown, discovering her inborn powers over the elements, and the natives had come to revere her as their goddess.

"Wh-who are you, stranger?" she asked the

bald man in the wheelchair who sat facing her, looking at her with eyes of blazing intensity. "What business have you in Ororo's land?"

"I am called Xavier—Professor Charles Xavier," the stranger told her. "And I have come to make you an offer I pray you will not refuse."

"An...offer?" Ororo echoed. "What have you to offer a goddess?"

The stranger wheeled himself closer, his gaze fixing her in place, freezing her to the spot. "You have a land, Ororo," he said softly, "and people who adore you. I offer you a world—and people who may fear you, but people who need you nonetheless. The world I offer is not beautiful, but it is real—far more real than the fantasy you're living now."

She could feel her heart racing as the words of the stranger cut through her, stabbing her with the truth.

"You are no goddess, Ororo. You are a mutant—and you have responsibilities. I ask you to leave your home and your exalted status here, to fulfill the purpose for which your life was intended—the protection and salvation, not of a single tribe, but of all mankind!

"Come with me, child," the stranger said, reaching out his hand. "Taste the world outside. You may find its flavor bitter—or surprisingly sweet."

Ororo felt her mind whirling, but all the while she knew what her answer must be. "You present a most peculiar argument," she told the stranger. "Yet I sense a deep sincerity in your words. All right. I will...come with you. Perhaps the time has come for me to leave the nest at last."

In a splendid garden outside Osaka, Japan, two men sat, drinking tea together, looking for all the world like old friends. One was the owner of this estate—Shiro Yoshida. The other—Professor Charles Xavier.

Yoshida looked the professor over with eyes full of suspicion. He had been burned before, and the past was still all too alive inside him.

"I know your feelings toward the Western world," Xavier was saying. "And I would not have come to you—"

Yoshida finished the professor's sentence for him. "But you require help that only I may give. Is it not so, Professor?"

Xavier nodded solemnly, sipping once more on his tea.

"So!" Yoshida growled. "So, that is how it is." He looked the professor up and down, remembering his past encounters with the world of mutants—a world he had shunned ever since.

"I owe you nothing, Professor," Yoshida told his guest, making his feelings perfectly clear. "But," he added, rising to his feet, "perhaps I owe something to myself..."

At that, he removed his red satin robe, revealing the red-and-white striped uniform he wore underneath. Reaching into the pocket of the robe, he brought out a red-and-yellow mask, donning it slowly.

"Perhaps," he said, flexing his incredible mutant muscles, "perhaps it is time once more for the world to hear from—Sunfire!"

CHAPTER THREE

THE TEAM IS COMPLETE

Deep in the heart of the Russian steppes, near the shores of Lake Baikal, in Siberia, lay the Ust-Ordynski Collective Farm. There, the workers toiled year in and year out, providing the crops of grain that fed the Russian masses.

This year, the crop had been better than normal. The fields of wheat stretched to the horizon like an amber sea, waving in the wind that blew across the vast steppes.

The workers who toiled in the fields were filled with satisfaction as they labored to bring in the bountiful harvest. The fullness that comes with the knowledge of a job well done was theirs. And no one was more satisfied than Peter—or Piotr, as his Russian comrades called him—Rasputin, the collective farm's best worker.

Today, he stood in the center of the fields, his pitchfork in his hands, hoisting the harvested wheat into the combine as his little sister sat a distance away, playing with the doll he had woven for her out of used stalks.

Peter was lost in his work, in the power of his muscles, in the rhythm of his labor, and he was happy. Happy, that is, until...

"Peter!" the man in the combine shouted suddenly, pointing across the field. "Look! Your sister—!"

"What is—?" Peter looked up.

He took in the whole scene in an instant: the runaway tractor barreling down the hillside—the innocent child, his beloved sister, playing blindly in its path..."No!" he cried out in alarm, his eyes growing wide with horror.

Without hesitation, Peter Rasputin broke

into a run, his legs pumping, his heart pounding, the very air around him crackling with the energy of his exertion—energy released in a most astonishing manner.

For as he ran, his muscled frame, so like iron to begin with, was suddenly transformed into *real* metal! The worker who was the pride of his collective farm literally became a *man of steel*.

As the massive machine bore down relentlessly upon the unwitting child, the sprinting farmer snatched her from its path at the last possible moment!

There was no time for Peter Rasputin to move out of harm's way. So he simply stood his ground as the speeding tractor plunged toward him.

With one arm around his sister, he clenched his other hand into a fist, smashing it into the tractor with all his superhuman strength. The machine exploded into bits, which flew in all directions, as the blast echoed to the far horizons.

Peter Rasputin stood there, his startled sis-

ter safe in his arms, and felt himself torn by conflicting emotions. On the one hand, he was overjoyed that his sister was alive, that he had been able to save her from a horrible demise. On the other hand, he wondered how his beloved neighbors, poor as they were, would ever be able to afford another tractor.

That, though, was a worry for another day. This day would be filled with problems enough. For how was he to explain to his friends and neighbors what had happened? Never before had they seen him transformed into his other, secret self—the dual identity he had kept hidden from them all these years.

He looked over at his neighbors, who were keeping a safe distance from the man they thought they had known so well, the man who only now was returning from his metallic state to his more familiar one of flesh and blood.

And then he heard a voice in his head. A voice not his own..."Peter Rasputin," it said, so distinctly that he was amazed when no one else seemed to hear it. "I wish to talk to you."

Peter turned, first one way, then another,

but saw no one. Putting his sister down, he walked off toward the equipment shed, the voice in his head leading him mysteriously onward and away from the probing eyes of his friends and neighbors, eyes that would never truly understand him.

And there, inside the shed, someone was indeed waiting for him. A bald man in a wheelchair, who now spoke out loud in the very same voice that had spoken to him telepathically.

Professor Charles Xavier introduced himself and explained why he had come. His words were few, but were most persuasive.

"So," Peter Rasputin said when the man in the wheelchair had finished. "So, you want me to go with you...to America? But if I possess such power as you say—does it not belong to the state? To Russia, my mother country?"

The professor smiled knowingly at him. "Peter," he replied, "powers such as yours belong to the world—to be used for the good of all. And believe me, your powers are needed."

Peter nodded. "Come," he told his visitor. "We will talk of this with my parents."

Taking the handles of the professor's wheelchair, Peter guided him to the hut where his family lived, on the edge of the communal village. It was a simple wooden structure, with only a few pieces of furniture, but to Peter Rasputin, it was home—not at all an easy place to leave.

The star worker of the Ust-Ordynski Collective Farm explained to his beloved family who the professor was, and why he had come.

"And so," he concluded, "the professor wants to take me with him—to teach me how to deal with my...my mutant powers. Th-there is wisdom in his words, Papa," he said haltingly, his heart filled with conflicting emotions. "But I am happy here. Tell me, Papa—what should I do?"

Peter's aging father stood facing his son, his arms around Peter's mother. Their eyes were filled with tears, but they stood tall, unafraid of the moment they had always suspected would arrive.

"You must do as your inner heart tells you, my son," Peter's father said solemnly. "It will not betray you, I promise."

Peter swallowed hard, fighting back the emotions that threatened to overwhelm him. "My heart tells me to stay, Papa," he said. "But my conscience tells me otherwise. I must go," he said, turning to hug his tearful mother.

His father nodded slowly. "Then it is right that you do, my son," he said, joining the family embrace.

Little more than an hour later, Peter Rasputin and the professor were ready to depart. Across the field lay the odd-looking jet that had brought the stranger to the Russian heartland.

Turning back once more to his family, Peter waved goodbye.

"*Dosvidanya*, Peter," his mother called to him. "Never forget—our love goes with you."

"Do not worry, Mama," Peter shouted. "I will write you. Good-bye, Papa—I will make you both proud. You'll see!"

Through his tears, his father nodded, and waved one last time. "We are already proud... my son," he said.

John Proudstar did not like living on the reservation at Camp Verde, Arizona. He did not like to watch the old ones, sitting slumped against their doorsteps, dreaming dreams of glory long gone.

John Proudstar was an Apache—and he was ashamed of what his people had become.

The Apache were meant to be hunters, warriors—not sad-eyed and self-pitying. They were meant to run free through the white sands of the desert, the wind blowing wildly through their hair.

So thought John Proudstar as he stalked the deer ahead of him, racing after it with speed no human on earth could match and bringing it down with a power no one else knew he had.

Once, he told himself, nothing could stand before the Apache. The deer that had covered this land fell by the score before Apache skill, Apache bravery...

But never, he knew, had any deer fallen like this—with one lone man chasing it on foot and wrestling it to the ground by its antlers!

"There, noble beast—do you see?" he cried out to the vanquished animal. "There is still a warrior among the Apache!"

The deer did not stir. Instead, a strange voice inside his head answered him.

"And such a man have I come looking for, John Proudstar," the voice said.

"Huh?" Confused, the panting Apache turned around, to see the strangest sight he had ever laid eyes on.

"How in blazes did a guy in a wheelchair get way out here in the wilderness?" he asked. "Not that it matters much," he added, the customary chip on his shoulder returning with a vengeance. "You've got five seconds to vamoose, white man! I don't want company—especially yours!"

"Don't be too hasty, my young friend," the white stranger said, still not opening his mouth. The voice echoed inside John Proudstar's head, confusing him. Where did the stranger get such a mysterious power?

"I've come to help you fulfill your dream,"

the stranger said, finally speaking out loud. "To give pride back to your people. You are special, John Proudstar. You are a mutant—and you are needed."

"And you can chew a cactus, mister," Proudstar replied, his temper rising. "The white man needs me? That's tough! I owe him nothing but the grief he's given my people! Now beat it!"

Proudstar turned his back on the stranger and started to walk away into the desert. But the stranger's voice followed after him, still ringing in his ears.

"I offer you a chance to help the world—and you turn your back on me?" the stranger remarked. "Then perhaps what you say is true—perhaps the Apache have become frightened, selfish children!"

The words struck John Proudstar like a slap across the face. "Ho-kay... that does it," he growled, turning back to face his tormentor. "Ain't nobody that calls me a coward, mister. I'm as good as the next guy—heck, I'm better! You give me a chance and I'll prove it!"

The stranger was smiling now, nodding his head in approval. "And you will have your chance, John Proudstar," he said quietly. "I promise you that."

"I have gathered the new team together," Professor Xavier telepathically informed his red-visored friend, who was waiting back at Headquarters for his arrival. "Make all the necessary preparations."

As they flew back toward Westchester County on the Blackbird, Professor Charles Xavier cast a doubtful eye over his new recruits. Already, they had begun to argue among themselves. Sunfire, Wolverine, and John Proudstar were each difficult to get along with, to say the least. Would they ever be able to operate as a team?

Most important, would any of them, his new X-Men, be equal to the task that lay before them? he wondered. Or would they carry the whole world down with them into ruin?

CHAPTER FOUR

VANISHED!

After the new recruits arrived, the school had at first seemed a latter-day Tower of Babel. Each mutant knew how to speak only his or her own language. But fortunately, a telepathic crash course in the English language had closed the communication gap in mere minutes.

Now, Professor Charles Xavier sat somberly studying his colorfully costumed houseguests.

"In all my life," said Peter Rasputin, "such clothing as this I have never seen!"

"The costume is beautiful," Ororo gasped

in wonder. "And the fit—perfect! But how did you—?"

"The uniforms," Professor Xavier informed them all, "are constructed from unstable molecules, which adjust themselves where necessary. But right now, while we are all together, let me explain more fully why I have brought you here."

The seven mutants gathered around him, casting doubtful, even hostile, looks at each other. Only Sunfire and Banshee had been here before, and Sunfire's memories of that time were anything but pleasant.

"First of all," the professor began, "you should know that, although I am known to the world only as a respected scientist, I, too, am a mutant.

"My powers are mainly telepathic, but not totally. I can, if necessary, send out mental energy bolts that can knock out an enemy or hypnotize him. I mention this," he added wryly, "for those of you who, perhaps, respect only force of the physical kind." He paused and gave Wolverine and John Proudstar a pointed look before he went on.

"Long ago, I realized that there was going to be trouble on Earth between 'normal' humans and the growing numbers of mutants with superpowers. I knew 'normal' people would fear mutants. So I decided to pledge my life to the cause of helping mankind and mutantkind to live together in peace.

"Unfortunately, there was a complicating factor. Not all mutants are good, no more than all humans are good. There are some evil mutants who want to rule the earth and make humans into slaves.

"So I decided to recruit a team of mutants that would fight off all these threats, and who would become the champions of both mankind and other good mutants. I called this team the 'X-Men.'

"I brought them here with the help of this computer behind me. I call it Cerebro—it can detect and identify mutant activity anywhere in the world, anywhere in the galaxy, for that matter. It helped me find the original X-Men, and I brought them here, to my so-called

'School for Gifted Youngsters.' I trained them, molded them into a team, and sent them into action. They did quite well, too. That is, until–"

"Until what, Professor?" Wolverine demanded. "What happened?"

"Yeah, prof," John Proudstar spoke up. "What's the dope here? Forget this gifted youngsters stuff. Why have you brought us all to this crazy place? Give us the real story, or we're outta here right now!"

"Right now," Sunfire echoed, "you will tell us why you dragged us here, Professor! I, for one, am swiftly losing my patience!"

"Sunfire, please..." Professor Xavier sighed sadly. "It was not my intention to waste your time." He had known his task would be difficult, but this was proving even harder than he had imagined. It was time to bring out the heavy artillery.

"I want you to meet someone who can explain the situation far better than I. My friends, allow me to present Scott Summers— the man called Cyclops!"

The doors to the room burst open, and there stood the red-visored man. His blue and yellow uniform covered his tightly muscled body and his visor shielded the mutant eyes that were his awe-inspiring weapon.

"He will fill you in on the details of your mission, my new X-Men," Professor Xavier said. Then he sat back in his wheelchair and, like the others, turned his attention to Cyclops.

"The 'details,' people, are depressingly simple," Cyclops told them. "You have been called here because—the original X-Men have disappeared!"

He cast his glance around the room, taking in the seven mutants who had been gathered from the far-flung corners of the Earth. The new arrivals looked uneasily at each other, as if suddenly realizing the gravity of the moment

"You seven are our only hope of..." Suddenly, Cyclops stopped himself in mid-sentence. "But I'm getting ahead of myself," he said. "Come on. I may as well show you where it all began."

He took them over to the machine called Cerebro and said, "It was through this mechanism that we discovered all of you...and lost my closest friends.

"We'd all answered the signal-alarm within seconds that day—the professor, Angel, Iceman, my beloved Jean Grey, Polaris, my brother Havok, and myself. We couldn't understand it—Cerebro had never reacted so violently before.

"Apparently, the mechanism had detected a new mutant on the island of Krakoa in the South Pacific—a mutant so powerful as to defy classification!

"It seemed that we all had our work cut out for us—we had to find that mutant quickly, before someone else found it first!

"Soon, we were off to the South Pacific in our specially designed stratojet, the Blackbird—I think you're all familiar with it by now—arcing high over the brilliant blue water, streaking toward an unknown confrontation...

"I remember that we were all a little distracted on that trip. For our companion, Beast, was no longer with us. Beast had graduated from the school and no longer had any time for our struggle. We knew that we were sorely going to miss his incredible powers. But I reminded the other X-Men that right then we had business of our own to worry about. Krakoa loomed dead ahead, and with it, our destiny...

"It was a desolate-looking place. A 'mud-bar,' Iceman called it. But there was no time for discussion as we strapped in for landing. We touched down moments later, our VTOL jets lowering us gently to the ground, as gently as an infant is lowered into its cradle.

"But we were not infants, and this was definitely no child's game. All the insects in the air...the overgrown jungle...we were all feeling nervous. Iceman made a few jokes. I told him to shut up and shelve the snappy patter.

"When I think back on it now, I'm sorry I spoke to him so sharply. But at the time, I wasn't thinking about friendship—we had a difficult job ahead of us, finding that new mutant. It might even be an impossible task,

considering we had no idea what we were looking for.

"I decided we should fan out to see if we could locate the new mutant. But just then, Polaris cried out, warning us to look behind us. Havok shouted for us all to scatter, to get moving before we—"

Cyclops heaved a shuddering sigh. "I'm ashamed to say I never even saw what hit us," he admitted. "There was a huge explosion, and a greenish light blinded me. My head was a throbbing mass of pain and screaming images when I struggled awake, Lord knows how long afterward.

"I didn't realize where I was, nor did I really care. All that concerned me was my friends. What had happened to the other X-Men? Was Jean okay? I wondered. And worse—what had happened to me?

"My eyes were uncovered! They were normal—powerless! However hard I tried, I couldn't project my optic blasts!

"I looked around in confusion and panic. And that's when I discovered I was back on the Blackbird—and I wasn't in control! The automatic pilot was jammed. No matter what I did, I couldn't turn the craft back to the island!

"I spent the next five minutes pounding futilely on the control panel, then resigned myself to the situation and sat back in my seat. I wasn't happy by the time I reached Westchester—not happy at all.

"I explained to the professor what had happened, or at least as much as I knew. But what I knew wasn't much—only that something on Krakoa had taken away my powers and deposited me back in the stratojet.

"That's when I noticed the professor looking at me kind of funny. Seconds later, I knew why. My eyes were glowing again—stronger than ever. The professor warned me to grab some protective lenses and cover my eyes, but it was too late.

"I begged the heavens not to let it happen to me again, but I should have known better than to ask. The optic energies that had cursed me since my early teens were back again—with a vengeance. This time they were so strong that even *I* could not control them.

"The first blast blew me clear across the room. And the blasts just kept on getting stronger. Finally, the professor modified one of my old ruby quartz visors to contain my increased power. Then he left me here to retrain myself while he went in search of all of you."

A low murmur rose from the new team of X-Men.

"And he found us!" Wolverine growled. "So now what?"

"So now," Cyclops replied, "we go back to Krakoa to find the original X-Men—and the mutant that defeated us!"

"Incorrect, Cyclops!" Sunfire broke in. "Now *you* go back to Krakoa—not I! I will have no part in this fool's errand!"

"What—?" Cyclops said, taken aback by the violence of Sunfire's anger. "I don't understand—we offer you a chance to help your fellow mutants and—"

"I don't even *like* my fellow mutants, Cyclops," Sunfire spat. "I certainly will not risk my life to help them!"

Cyclops shook his head slowly, stepping back from confrontation, although he would have liked to belt Sunfire one right then and there.

"I feel sorry for you, Sunfire," he said. "But I don't have time to waste arguing. The rest of us have a job to do—and we're going to do it!"

Shortly afterward, Cyclops, together with six of the seven new X-Men, boarded the Blackbird and flew swiftly toward the sky.

All of them were silent, their gazes inexorably drawn to the one empty seat on board.

Ororo, now code-named Storm by the

professor, was the first to speak. "It seems I have had my first taste of mutant camaraderie," she said sardonically. "And I must say, Cyclops—I did not like it."

She was answered by a snort from John Proudstar. "Maybe you didn't notice, sister, but this group ain't exactly a mutual admiration society! We're all involved in this fiasco for our own reasons, girly," he growled as their stratojet streaked over the Pacific Ocean. "And patting each other on the back ain't one of—huh?"

He broke off suddenly, turning to look out the window. "Hey, one-eye," he called out, alarm rising in his voice. "Don't look now, but there's something followin' us!"

"You're right!" Cyclops gasped, staring at the red streak in the sky rapidly gaining on the Blackbird. "Everyone to battle stations!"

CHAPTER FIVE

THE JOURNEY

They had hardly begun to know one another's powers, let alone to work together as a team. If the red streak were a threat, how would they deal with it? As the streak came ever closer to the stratojet, each mutant wondered what the others were planning.

"Wait!" Wolverine shouted, his keen eyes picking out the form as it grew nearer. "Well, I'll be jiggered," he said to Cyclops. "If it's not our Japanese friend!"

Sure enough, it was Sunfire. "Are you going to open the hatch, Cyclops?" he roared from outside. "Or do you expect me to fly all the way to Krakoa by myself?"

In no time, the hatch was opened and the eighth member of their team had occupied the last empty chair on board the Blackbird.

"So," Kurt Wagner, now known as Nightcrawler, said. "The prodigal mutant returns! Why did you change your mind, Sunfire? Afraid to go home alone?"

The face underneath the horned red mask was expressionless, but the gritted teeth told the whole story. "My reasons are nobody's business but my own, misfit!" Sunfire growled. "You'd do well to remember that!"

An hour passed, two hours...until the forsaken island called Krakoa loomed full before the viewports.

"So that's where you mislaid your partners, huh?" Thunderbird asked Cyclops.

"Can't say much for your taste in vacation spots, Summers," Wolverine chimed in.

Cyclops turned his visored gaze toward his hostile companion. "And I can't say much for your sense of humor, Wolverine. Nor yours, Thunderbird," he added.

"The name is Proudstar, one-eye!" the Apache mutant shot back.

"Not anymore," Cyclops told him in no uncertain terms. "The professor has given you all code names, group. You might as well start getting used to them."

Drawing them together in the cockpit, Cyclops laid out their plan of attack. "Now, the assault teams will be as follows—Storm, you and Colossus will come in from the north."

Ororo looked at the man she'd only recently come to know as Peter Rasputin, and nodded. She liked Colossus, his openness and his goodness of heart And she could tell that the regard was mutual.

"Banshee and Wolverine will move across from the east," Cyclops went on.

"'Tis a pleasure ta be workin' with ye, laddie," Banshee said, with a smile at his new partner.

But Wolverine did not return the grin. "Whoopee," was all he said.

"Sunfire and Nightcrawler will start searching from the south," Cyclops continued.

"No—not him!" Sunfire groaned, agonized that his new partner was the man he'd nearly come to blows with not two hours ago.

"I did not hear Cyclops giving you a choice, man," Nightcrawler answered.

"Thunderbird and I will handle the west end of the island," Cyclops finished. "Now get ready, south team—your drop is coming up!"

"I don't much like the tone of your voice, Cyclops," Sunfire griped.

"We can argue about it when you get back," Cyclops said firmly. "Now, go!"

The hatch opened, and Sunfire and Nightcrawler were gone, their hands linked as they floated to earth, aided by Sunfire's flying ability.

"East team—go!" Cyclops shouted, and off went Wolverine and Banshee.

As they dropped, Banshee's wild wail sounded, shattering the air around them.

"Cripes!" Wolverine shouted. "Do you have to screech like that?" His only answer was a mischievous smile from his new partner.

Back on the Blackbird, Cyclops called out "North team!"

"That is our signal, Storm," Colossus said, leaning over the open hatch.

"Colossus, no!" Storm yelled as her partner suddenly leaped from the plane. "You fool— you cannot fly!"

As they dropped toward the island, Colossus turned to her with a wide grin. "Of course not," he shouted. "But I can land with the best of them!"

On the stratojet, Thunderbird looked down to the north. "The chick and the Russky have landed," he told Cyclops. "And it looks like they're arguing—which is about par for this outfit!"

"We're going down next, Thunderbird," Cyclops told him. "Strap in!"

Once more, the stratojet's VTOL system lowered the craft to earth. And though he tried, the man called Cyclops could not suppress a shudder. How many more would they lose this time? he wondered morbidly. Would he even live long enough to find out?

But he was a professional, this star-crossed mutant. The questions followed him as he stepped out upon the landscape—but he left his fear behind him in the ship.

"East is that way, Thunderbird," he said,

pointing in that direction. "And the sooner we get started, the sooner we'll get there."

"Yes sir, General One-eye, sir!" came the sardonic reply, complete with mock salute. "I just hope you're not leading me into another Little Big Horn! It'd be just my luck to be the first Indian to get massacred by—"

His words were interrupted by a moan from Cyclops. "Hold it! The mini-Cerebro. We need it to sense any mutant activity on the island! And I left it back in—huh?"

Looking back, Cyclops let out a gasp of amazement. "I don't believe it!"

"Don't believe what?" Thunderbird asked.

"The Blackbird!" Cyclops replied. "It's gone!"

"But that's impossible!" Thunderbird sputtered, not believing what he wasn't seeing. "The ground doesn't just open up and swallow a jet plane whole!"

"Absolutely right," Cyclops confirmed, turning back around toward the east. "And strange temples don't suddenly spring up out of nowhere—but one has!"

Thunderbird spun around, only to have his eyes confront the unbelievable. There, rising above the thick jungle, was a gigantic temple where none had been before!

"Huh? That joint wasn't there when we landed," Thunderbird said in awe.

"Exactly," Cyclops agreed. "And since it seems as good a spot as any to start searching, let's go!"

Grumbling in annoyance, the mutant now reluctantly called Thunderbird followed his companion into the verdant underbrush. John Proudstar had never much liked the jungle—and apparently, the feeling was mutual. For no sooner had he stepped in among the undergrowth than he felt something thick and superstrong grab him around the throat!

"These vines!" he gasped, clutching at the tendrils that gripped him more tightly every second. "They're alive!"

"A condition we won't share much longer," panted Cyclops, himself now caught up in the attacking shrubbery, "unless we do something—fast!"

CHAPTER SIX

....

STRANGE ENCOUNTERS

"Got any suggestions in particular, one-eye?" Thunderbird asked, managing to free himself from the grasp of the gigantic vines. He skill fully swung from the plant ropes while he tied three of them in a huge knot.

"Not really, Thunderbird," Cyclops shot back. Pressing the button that opened his red visor, he sent forth an optic blast, shattering an attacking vine into slimy green pieces. "For a beginner, you're doing pretty well on your own!"

Within moments, the two young X-Men, newly appreciative of each others' abilities, had left the strangling creeper vines far behind them. And the trail of devastation littering the ground left little doubt which way they had gone.

Minutes later, they found themselves at the enormous stone gates of the temple. "Well," Cyclops said, looking up at the vastness of the ancient structure before them, "we've made it in reasonable shape. I wonder how the others are faring..."

On the island's east side, Wolverine and Banshee had landed, only to find themselves attacked by a troop of giant crabs!

"Saints, laddie!" Banshee cried out. "Will ye look at the size o' them beasties! They're as big as houses, every last one of 'em!"

"Looks like the local welcoming committee, Irish," Wolverine said, with his typical black humor. "But a handshake from one of them can be fatal!"

With a nod to his new partner, Wolverine

threw himself at his attackers. "Good thing, then, they're not the only ones around here with big, sharp claws, isn't it?" he called out as he slashed away with his adamantium appendages, slicing through the shell and flesh of the first crab in his way. "The Wolverine has claws of his own—and he likes to use them!"

Then, turning back to his companion, he added, "Hey—are you just going to stand around gawking, Irish, or are you going to help me?"

But the Erin-born mutant was already aloft —and though his sonic scream was not nearly so flamboyant as his companion's slashing talons, it was nonetheless equally effective. One after the other, the giant crabs began exploding in pieces on the shore, shattered by the focused beam of sound.

The battle was violent, but brief. "Well, laddie," Banshee said cheerfully as he and Wolverine surveyed the corpses of their attackers littering the shore, "sure'n it looks like we've done fer the beasties! We'd best be gettin' on to that temple we spied as we were landin' here."

"Yeah. Sure," Wolverine agreed. "There's nothing to keep us here—anymore."

Meanwhile, on the island's northern shore, Storm gazed into the distance at a surprising sight. "Odd," she said to her companion, "I do not recall seeing that temple before. Come, Colossus—let us begin our search there."

"Whatever you say, Ororo," he agreed as they set off through a steep, narrow canyon, surrounded by looming cliffs. As they walked, he regarded her with undisguised admiration. "You are so unlike the women in my—"

Suddenly, he stopped, alert in every fiber of his being. "Eh? What's that sound?" he asked.

Both of them now looked up as the distant rumbling grew ever louder and nearer. "An avalanche!" Storm cried out. "Quickly, Colossus—perhaps we can still outrun it!"

The two of them took off at breakneck speed, faster than any normal human could possibly have traveled. But no matter how fast they ran, the tumbling rocks kept getting closer and closer to them!

Cursing in his native Russian, Colossus called out to his partner, "This landslide cannot be outrun, Ororo—it has changed its direction to follow us!"

Turning, and slowing to a halt, Storm saw that it was true. "Then if we cannot avoid a confrontation," she said soberly, "we must stand our ground and defend ourselves!"

"Those mad rocks can no longer hurt me, Ororo," Colossus announced as his body transformed itself into its invincible metallic form. "But for threatening you," he added, hoisting a huge, dead tree trunk in his hands, "I shall crush them!"

And swinging the enormous trunk as if it were a baseball bat, he swatted at the rocks, pulverizing them one after the other with the sheer force of his blows!

"I thank you, Peter," Storm called to him. "But there is no need to protect me—I am no longer threatened."

Colossus turned and saw that she was right. Using her powers over nature, Storm had conjured the four winds to come to her aid. They came together in a swirling vortex, lifting the heavy boulders right off the ground, gathering them into a huge column, and sending them flying off seaward. There they shot into the ocean, sending up a tower of spray as they sank to the bottom.

Shortly afterward, the two found their way to the temple, where they met up with Banshee and Wolverine, Cyclops and Thunderbird.

"Storm...Colossus," Cyclops greeted them.

"Glad you made it in one piece!"

"Barely, Cyclops...just barely," Storm replied.

"Faith!" Banshee said, smiling. "'Tis good t'be seein' ye all again. 'Twas a moment there I had me doubts."

"And you were not alone," Storm confessed. "I only hope the others arrive safely as well."

"Yes," Cyclops agreed, his expression darkening. "They should have been here by now..."

CHAPTER SEVEN

THE MYSTERIOUS TEMPLE

Meanwhile...off to the south, Nightcrawler and Sunfire were engaged in a battle for their lives—a battle against a flock of gigantic birds of prey!

"These birds seem determined to prevent us from reaching that strange temple ahead, Sunfire," Nightcrawler remarked as he grappled simultaneously with three of the vicious creatures—one in each hand and a third grasped in his coiling, strangling tail.

"A remarkable observation, misfit!" Sunfire shot back with his usual bitterness as he unleashed solar blasts at his opponents, obliterating them one after another. "You have a positive talent for stating the obvious!"

"Your sarcasm is uncalled for, Sunfire," Nightcrawler told his reluctant partner. "I begin to think the mutant community is no more hospitable than the human—"

"*Skreee!*" one of the birds shrieked as it swooped down for a surprise attack on Nightcrawler, who was looking in the opposite direction. Gasping in surprise, Nightcrawler cut short his remarks just in time.

Just as the bird was about to rake him with its talons, there came a burst of flame, the stench of brimstone—and the mutant called Nightcrawler was suddenly elsewhere! His laugh of triumph was a hideous howl as the bewildered bird went tumbling earthward.

"Your manner seems much like that of the beasts you so resemble, misfit," Sunfire called to him. "How appropriate! But Sunfire has no need of such parlor tricks as yours. I much prefer the direct approach." And he fired solar bolts in two directions at once, sending a pair of the attacking creatures to a fiery doom.

Nightcrawler looked around at the suddenly empty skies above them. "Your 'direct approach,' it appears, has left us without opponents, Sunfire," he remarked, offering a compliment to his partner as a way of making peace.

"I suggest," said Sunfire, unappeased, "that we get on to that temple, misfit—assuming, of course, you can keep up with me."

Minutes later, they arrived at the temple gates, where the six remaining members of their team awaited them.

"Cyclops!" Nightcrawler called out. "Have we kept you waiting long?"

"Not at all," their leader replied. "We just got here ourselves. And since we are all finally here," he added, rising and turning to face the great stone doors which barred their way into the building itself, "I think it's about time we found out what's inside this tumbledown temple! I've got a gut feeling someone lured us here for precisely that purpose—and I'd hate to disappoint them now!"

Cautiously, Cyclops and the seven new X-Men approached the stone doors. Together, they went over every inch of the stone facing, searching for a knob, a latch, or any other way of opening the doors. To no avail.

"It looks," said Cyclops, "as if we're going to have to earn the dubious privilege of getting in there. The door is sealed tight—and it's about a foot thick. Sunfire...Storm...Colossus. Looks like the time has come for your first practical lesson in the art of being an X-Man!"

The lesson was entitled "Breaking and Entering," and, although the neophyte X-Men lacked the finesse of their predecessors, they certainly got an "A" for effort. Colossus delivered a crushing blow to the stone, while Sunfire directed a solar blast at the doors, blowing them apart completely.

With her command of the winds, Storm got rid of the mountain of debris the other two had created, clearing the way for the new X-

Men to enter the ancient, mysterious temple.

Still slightly astonished by their own abilities, the young mutants stepped cautiously into the stygian darkness inside—and suddenly found their hearts swelling heavy in their throats!

"Oh...my...God..." Cyclops whispered hoarsely, his eyes filling with tears at the horrifying sight that greeted them as they adjusted to the darkness. "Oh, my dear God—"

Cyclops was too horrified to continue. There before him hung his comrades, the original X-Men, suspended in midair and surrounded by what looked to be vines similar to the type that had attacked Cyclops and

Thunderbird earlier. But *these* vines had attached themselves to the original X-Men with sucker-like tendrils and seemed to be siphoning the life force from their limp bodies!

"Well, don't just stand there staring at them!" Cyclops shouted to his new companions. "In pity's name—set them free!"

Instantly, the new team set to work as one, forgetting their differences in the urgency of the moment. But as they yanked the original X-Men free of the sucking tendrils, there was a sudden rumbling, so loud that they stopped dead in their tracks.

"Cripes!" Wolverine gasped. "What's going on? As soon as we pulled these tubes loose, the place started shaking itself apart!"

"Quickly, then," Cyclops ordered. "Carry whoever is closest to you—and let's get out of here before this temple comes down around our ears!"

And sure enough, as they ran outside, carrying the limp bodies of the original X-Men to safety, the sinister old temple shook violently, toppling into ruin behind them!

But there was no time to stand idly by watching the temple's demise. The new X-Men turned their attention to reviving their rescued teammates. Within a minute or two, the original team that had come to Krakoa began to show signs of renewed life.

"Hey," Cyclops said, a broad smile crossing his lips as he gazed down into the face of his adored Jean Grey. "They're coming around! Must not have been as bad as—"

But before he could finish, Angel, the first of the original team to regain consciousness, turned to him. "*Why*, Cyclops? Why did you come back for us?" he cried.

"Huh?" Cyclops stood there stunned, uncomprehending. He had thought they would be overjoyed to be rescued, happy that he had come back for them. He certainly hadn't expected this!

"You fool!" Angel shouted. "Don't you understand? *It* wanted you to come back—and bring others with you! It was all a trap—and now it's too late!"

Cyclops stared around him at the ruins of

the collapsed building. Even as he watched, the earth seemed to slowly swallow the remaining rubble. And now, the horrifying truth was beginning to dawn upon him. Now, when it was indeed, as Angel had said, too late...

"The ground—rearing up around the fallen temple?" he gasped.

"Of course!" Angel screamed. "Haven't you realized it yet? We came to this island to look for a mutant...but the mutant is *the island itself!*"

CHAPTER EIGHT

IT'S ALIVE!

The images flooded their mutant minds as they stood there, transfixed—images explaining everything, sent to them telepathically by the beast they now faced.

The sunburst brilliance of an early atomic test, whose unseen radiation permeated every living organism here, until they grew linked in a colony intelligence that gave the island a life of its own.

Krakoa grew hungry then—a hunger barely appeased when the X-Men arrived upon the scene. Krakoa fed upon their mutant energies and grew hungrier still. Thus, it released one

X-Man—Cyclops—and sent him forth to find more food.

The beast that was Krakoa, the island monster, now towered over them, its jaws drooling acidic ooze, its enormous eyes glaring down at its prey.

"And now," came its gravelly voice, the voice of billions of organisms linked together into one hideous whole, "now, we will go hungry no longer!"

Cyclops stared up at the towering beast that loomed above him, the anger rising in his throat. "Filthy monster!" he screamed at the top of his lungs. "You used me—like a lousy Judas goat leading lambs to the slaughter!"

The monster's laugh shook the ground that was a part of it. "Yes, we used you, eyeless one, as we used the crippled one who gathered you all together at the command of a voice only his mind could hear!"

The head, the size of a skyscraper, loomed down over them, gushing drool that sizzled as it dripped to the ground. "But the time for explanations is past!" the horrible voice announced. "Now it is time for Krakoa to feed!"

"Scatter, X-Men!" Cyclops called out to his troops. "Quickly—*uunngh!*" His orders were cut short by a sizzling blast that shot from the monster's eyes, sending Cyclops and those nearest him—Colossus, Jean Grey, and Thunderbird—flying backward through the air.

But not all the X-Men were ready to follow orders. Wolverine leapt forward toward the beast, his claws gleaming. "You lily-livers want to scatter, that's swell," he roared, slashing at blinding speed at the woody flesh of Krakoa, "but Wolverine is going for blood!"

If the vegetal monstrosity had any blood to

lose, though, it gave no evidence of the fact.

Angel, hovering overhead with his wings outstretched, called out to his once and future companion, "Your solar blasts have no effect on the thing, Sunfire!"

"Nor do my bolts of lightning!" cried Storm, streaking through the sky near Angel. "But we must fight on, whatever the risk!"

Unbelievably, but true enough, the monster that was Krakoa Island seemed all but impervious to the combined superhuman powers of the X-Men! The battle that was now joined was a flurry of sheer unbridled savagery—for none of them, new or old, had ever come up against such a foe.

The conflict went on and on without resolution, except that the thirteen X-Men were collecting numerous bumps and bruises. How much longer could they hold out against a far worse fate?

Then, suddenly, Cyclops stopped dead in his tracks as the face of Professor X loomed large before him in his mind's eye.

"Scott—stop!" the familiar telepathic voice

commanded him. "You're going about this all wrong!"

"Huh? Professor...?" Cyclops dodged a lunging attack from the gaping maw of Krakoa. Its sharp, enormous teeth gnashed, narrowly missing a mutant meal.

"I've been mentally monitoring your battle thus far," the telepathic voice informed Cyclops while the other X-Men distracted Krakoa. "Studying this living island...and I believe I've discovered its sole weak point! Now this is my plan..."

In an instant, Professor Charles Xavier's mental commands were projected halfway around the world. Then, the professor closed his eyes, steeling himself for the coming ordeal. In moments, his concentration was total—and an even more intense battle began!

It was a war fought on two fronts—as Professor X waged deadly mental combat with a crazed communal intellect—while his students raced to carry out his plan...

One by one, Cyclops communicated the professor's instructions to his fellow X-Men. At his command, the eyes of the mutant called Storm grew dark once more, and she soared aloft on the wings of the wind.

High above Krakoa she hovered, slowly summoning the tempest's full electric fury— then suddenly transmitting those seething energies to the lithe young woman who waited anxiously below, thus restoring the mighty magnetic powers of the girl called Lorna Dane—otherwise known as Polaris!

Within moments, the circuit was completed, and Lorna Dane screamed in anguish as her physical limits were reached—and *exceeded!*

"Don't stop!" she screamed in agony and triumph as she felt the surge of power course through her body and mind.

And Alex Summers, also known as Havok—the man who loved her, who had loved Lorna Dane since the moment he'd laid eyes on her, turned away from the fight, unable to bear the pain of seeing the woman he loved tortured so.

Running up to his brother, Scott, he grabbed him by the shoulders and spun him around to face him. "You've got to call it off, Scott!" he demanded of his older brother. "Lorna can't take that kind of punishment—she'll be killed!"

Cyclops stared back at his brother solemnly, knowing the pain this was causing Havok, yet unwilling and unable to stop it. "Alex, I can't," he reluctantly told him. "I can't sacrifice a world to save one woman, Alex—even if she is the woman you love!"

Havok's eyes clouded over with pain and anger, and his fingers dug into his brother's shoulder, making Cyclops wince with pain. "I swear to you," Havok hissed. "Brother or no brother—if she dies..."

The remainder of Havok's outburst was drowned out by the crackling roar of the downpour created by Storm's exertions. Thunder rolled and lightning sizzled all around the exhausted X-Men as they stood for a moment in silence, watching the awesome forces of nature at work. But then a horrifying realization began to dawn on one superhero after another. In her effort to energize and empower

Polaris, Storm had also inadvertently given new life to their tiring enemy!

"Begorra!" Banshee gasped as Krakoa reared back, fresh with new power. "The blinkin' beast is gettin' stronger now! But how...?"

As if in answer to Banshee's question, Cyclops heard the warning voice in his head, the voice that came to him from halfway around the world.

"Cyclops, the island's mind has suddenly grown more forceful," Professor X informed him. "The rain—I...I didn't factor in its effect on the monster..."

The voice was growing fainter now, and Cyclops could sense the professor's mental energies weakening.

Was it possible? Could the professor have made a fatal error in his calculations? In all the time he had known Professor Charles Xavier, Scott Summers had never known him to miscalculate—at least not like this!

"I...I can't maintain my assault any longer," the faltering voice in his head informed him. "Forgive me, Scott..." He could barely hear the professor now. "...but I fear...you're...on...your...own..."

The voice of their mentor was gone. Now, the only sound Cyclops could hear was the deafening roar of Krakoa as the monster, sensing victory, readied itself for its final, fatal assault.

"Fools!" it roared, and Cyclops could almost hear the hideous laughter behind the voice. "You brought rain from the sky to destroy us—but it serves only to replenish us—and give us the strength to destroy you!"

CHAPTER NINE

MAGNETIC APPEAL

Krakoa stood poised now to make an end of the X-Men. But as before, Professor Charles Xavier's mutant protégés were ready to argue that point—quite strongly! From every side, they attacked with all their remaining strength, distracting the island monster so that it could not prepare itself for what was to come.

Jean Grey stole a quick glance at Cyclops. "We can't hold that thing off forever, Scott," she informed him, stating the obvious. "If the professor's plan doesn't work..."

"We'll know if it works soon enough, Jean," Cyclops replied tersely. "Get everybody back—we're ready to begin!"

With that, a solemn Scott Summers turned, to find that the figure of Lorna Dane had become lost within a coruscating incandescent tower of sheer magnetic force.

His mutant eyes narrowed behind the red visor, and a single word formed upon his lips:

"NOW!"

With almost indescribable force, Lorna's magnetic energies erupted downward, through four thousand miles of the earth's molten interior, down, down to the very center of the planet itself—where its effects were immediate and violent!

The island monster that was Krakoa suddenly staggered backward, and the ground rumbled uncomfortably, sending the X-Men who stood upon it reeling.

"Wh-what is happening to us?" the gravelly voice of the monster rumbled. "Why do we feel so strange? Our mind hurts so...can't retain our humanoid form...! Please...please...help us..."

"It's working!" Cyclops cried out jubilantly. "Exactly as the professor said it would!" Turning to his companions, he added urgently, "We've only got seconds to clear out of here— before the end!"

But Havok was not listening. Alarmed for the safety of the woman he loved, he turned to find her, knowing she would need his help. "Lorna's too weak to run for it!" he shouted. "I'll—huh?"

To his surprise, Havok found that Lorna Dane, unconscious though she was, did not lack for help. Indeed, Iceman had already come to her aid, and she lay limp in his arms, much to the annoyance of Havok.

"The lady doesn't need your help, hot-shot!" Iceman told him. "She's in good hands for a change!"

Havok felt the flush of rage overcoming him, and he stepped forward, murder in his eyes. "Why, you little..." he began, only to be cut off by an urgent command from his older brother.

"We can argue later!" Cyclops ordered.

"Now just move it!"

And move it they did, as few other beings on Earth possibly could have, knowing that there were only seconds before it would be too late!

"Holy crow!" Thunderbird yelled as they raced for the shore. "Will ya take a look at the beach up ahead? This whole stinkin' island is breakin' up around us!"

It was true, as all of them could plainly see. Massive tree trunks split in two and crashed to the ground. Cracks hundreds of feet long opened in the earth, swallowing birds, ani-

mals, plants...The power of Polaris's awesome magnetic energies had done its work well—perhaps too well!

"Without our stratojet," Angel shouted anxiously, "there's no way we can get far enough from this island before—huh?"

His words were cut short by the shivering, cracking sound of water freezing at superfast speed. Iceman was using his mutant powers to freeze a patch of ocean, creating a raft of ice for them!

"Never let it be said we Icemen aren't good for something, Angel!" the jocular X-Man called out to his friend. "Everybody get aboard—and fast!"

Swiftly, the desperate X-Men clambered aboard the crude ice raft, then hung on for dear life as the mutant powers of Cyclops and Havok propelled the makeshift vessel away from Krakoa with the speed of a hurtling hydroplane!

Behind them, the world convulsed in carnage, as the results of Lorna Dane's energy-bolt became apparent at last.

For her electrically charged burst had cut across the planet's primary lines of magnetic force, severing them, and for an instant around the island of Krakoa—gravity ceased to exist!

Then the earth forces came violently back together—and the effect was the same as squeezing wet soap through a fist!

Krakoa shot heavenward at lightning speed, the roar of its violent separation from the earth drowned out by its agonized death-cries, which rang for long seconds in the minds of the awestruck X-Men as Krakoa disappeared into the sky, never to be seen again.

"Incredible," Wolverine gasped, unable to say more.

"If I hadn't of seen it with my own eyes, I wouldn't of believed it," Thunderbird said, impressed in spite of himself.

The X-Men, new and old, looked at each other in wonderment, almost shyly, and grins spread across their faces at the growing aware-ness of what they had just accomplished. Even Lorna Dane, beginning to recover now from the massive exertions that had rendered her unconscious, managed a smile, and she and Havok reached for each other in a warm embrace.

But their happiness was short-lived—and more than a bit premature. For now, a more frightening reality intruded upon the scene.

"Brace yourselves, everybody," Cyclops called out as the ice raft slowed down ominously and came to a halt, then started sliding backward on the surface of the sea. "There's trouble ahead. The ocean is rushing in to fill the space Krakoa just vacated—and we're caught in the whirlpool!"

CHAPTER TEN

THIRTEEN X-MEN?

Slowly at first, then faster and faster, the little ice raft carrying the bedraggled X-Men began circling the edges of the cavernous vortex, drawing closer and closer to the awful black hole at its center. There were only moments left to act!

"Quickly, Bobby!" Cyclops shouted, turning to Iceman. "Throw an airtight ice dome over this raft—it's our only chance to survive this miserable maelstrom!"

Nodding his understanding, Iceman did as

he was told, and seconds later, the X-Men found themselves surrounded by a hard, frigid, air-tight shell.

Not a moment too soon, either. For now, the great ice bubble was sucked down inexorably into the wildly swirling maw—and those within its shelter found themselves battered almost senseless against its cold, unfeeling walls by the awesome power of the raging sea.

Cries of pain sounded loudly within the frigid bubble as it reached the heart of the vortex—and then disappeared!

The X-Men were gone.

The seething waters closed above their heads, and the sea grew calm—ominously calm.

Interminable minutes passed, and still the surface of the sea remained untroubled. And then–

The huge gleaming bubble of ice burst through the surface of the ocean like a shiny white spaceship. It flew into the air, hovered there for a long moment, then landed hard on the surface, bobbing like a buoy in the middle of the endless sea.

From within that seemingly lifeless ball of ice, came a beam of scarlet fury that burst the bubble into a thousand jagged pieces.

And there, on their little raft, stood the X-Men, all thirteen of them, battered and bruised but, all things considered, none the worse for wear.

"Fresh air!" Jean Grey enthused. "Warm sun! Did you ever see anything more beautiful?"

"Yeah," Angel replied, stretching his wings and leaping off the raft to flutter above it. "That!" He pointed off to the west, where the sun was just about to set.

And there, bobbing on the surface of the sea, was the Blackbird!

"Almost forgot the ol' Blackbird was watertight!" Angel said with a laugh. "Paddle on over while I go open the hatch!"

Soon afterward, the stratojet was streaking across the night sky, homeward bound.

Inside, the X-Men, new and old, crowded around, all of them feeling the exhilaration of triumph, and the inexorable pull of togetherness—even those of them who wouldn't have admitted it a couple of hours earlier.

"Sorry we don't have seats for all of you," Cyclops remarked to the five X-Men who found themselves standing hunched uncomfortably together against the walls of the craft. "But this plane wasn't designed to carry so many mutants!"

"Which brings us to our next little problem," Banshee spoke up, looking around at his new companions. "How in the world are thirteen X-Men ever going to learn to get along together?"

"If being squeezed like sardines into this contraption doesn't bring us closer together, I don't know what will," growled Wolverine.

And the other twelve X-Men laughed as the Blackbird streaked off toward a bold new day—and a new beginning.

If you liked this book, here's a taste of...

Days of Future Past

Giant Sentinel robots were created by man to control mutants. In the future they have taken control of all mankind.

Kate Pryde, member of the renegade X-Men and one of the few surviving mutants, has a plan—a plan to project her mind back in time to a younger version of herself...

Kate paused, and took a deep breath. "Right now, in the future, I am an empty shell, a body without a soul. But here, in the present, I am meant to act. To prevent history, as I know it, from ever taking place."

"What will happen if you can't?" Angel, a fellow mutant and friend, asked.

"Then some of you will live," Kate told him. "But most of you will die."

BOOKS IN THIS SERIES

Days of Future Past

Second Genesis

Wolverine: Top Secret

The Xavier Files